Green Letters in the Cave

Ariel C. Cabasag, LPT, MATELL

Ukiyoto Publishing

All global publishing rights are held by

Ukiyoto Publishing

Published in 2025

Content Copyright © Ariel C. Cabasag
ISBN 9789370091009

All rights reserved.
No part of this publication may be reproduced, transmitted, or stored in a retrieval system, in any form by any means, electronic, mechanical, photocopying, recording or otherwise, without the prior permission of the publisher.

The moral rights of the author have been asserted.

This is a work of fiction. Names, characters, businesses, places, events, locales, and incidents are either the products of the author's imagination or used in a fictitious manner. Any resemblance to actual persons, living or dead, or actual events is purely coincidental.

This book is sold subject to the condition that it shall not by way of trade or otherwise, be lent, resold, hired out or otherwise circulated, without the publisher's prior consent, in any form of binding or cover other than that in which it is published.

www.ukiyoto.com

Acknowledgement

I truly acknowledged for publishing my English textbook. This is an indeed opportunity to work with company, where I could have shared my talents in writing, not only them but also, to the readers, who endlessly wish to acquire knowledge in English grammar. I understand that English structure can somewhat be arduous, due to proper way of using the language order in the sentences. This may not be a flawless book to guide you in writing the sentences correctly. However, this can be an impeccable book to inspire you, how imperative to engage in writing, with the integration of proper structure.

Sometimes English structure can't useful in dialogue, we admit that human beings could express the ideas freely without proper structure. However, we strongly believed that employing proper grammar could have helped us to tell the world, what we really want to be. Indeed, many speakers were able to convince people in accepting their ideas, thought it won't really acceptable to others. It's not just to be convincing, yet to use the language proficiently.

In conclusion, having a great foundation to use the language proficiently: this serves as a mirror to others, who are longing to immulate the essence of great language. To be use the language well: this inspires us to be a right bridge in the village.

Description

Unable to define how to live their lives meaningfully. Brimmed with boundless pain, dwelled their lives. However, as vibrant eyes discovered the letters in the cave, which answered their wishes, life became richer than before. The tree consists of ten leaves, which incredibly existed in the cave. Each leaf painted an indelible memory, which could alter the lives and souls.

It's been a trillion years since the poplar tree exists in Disneyland. Each leaf has metamorphosed life and wrenched minds onto radiant minds. Every time, the leaves crumble on the ground; there's one person who passed away in the town. The people hypothetically believed the tree, which leads to death without enough evidence. For a year, hundreds of folks die, which wobbles the teeth. However, nobody could assassinate the tree.

Inexhaustible million hands grasped the tree till the bough fell down the land. Instead of feeling chuffed shambling the land, however, their hands disabled. Thousands of eyes screamed how appalling their nights were.

As the dawn materialized in the sky, their crystal eyes gazed nothing on the land. Feeling so unbearable glimpsing at the way, though their hearts never got terrified of the daily dead in the town. But their hearts clasped the whole universe, and often felt mournful as the poplar tree had gone. Looking back, the folks relieved their whimpering days as they gaped at the leaf.

One day, feet sauntered on the green ground for the tearful eyes clenched the leaves. Unfortunately, their eyes unable to find it, what the eyes gazed at; the withered soil. It fell down their hearts, seeing in the past where lives were richer than today. Due to the occurrences, the folks got befuddled on how to make their lives richer and happier.

Life seemed awful in the village, as the poplar tree had gone. Most of their eyes fell down the river of tears, and put their eyes onto the sun. **There's a night when Cheryl's typhoon passed the entire Disneyland.** *Their hearts were joyfully attached to the rain, due to its cool hands healed their negativities, still the typhoon made the people float on the water.*

It's been ten nights of feeling appalling till their eyes glimpsed at a dead tree in the cave. Their hearts filled with crystal feelings knowing that fact the tree still saved them, no matter what they did to the tree before.

Endless eyes ascertained that the tree ceased in the cave. Their hearts seemed doleful while eyeing the shrivelled leaves. Instead of squealing their eyes onto the sea, they hugged the leaves, and promised to go back again in the cave. Their hearts deeply contemplate how bountiful trees were, being of their lives.

Their minds casted back how the poplar tree made their lives richer. The folks craved to trudge their feet in the cave again. It's been a decade of not visiting the cave, still a thousand people who have been longing to visit there.

There were ten nights which closed the entire universe; the folks got befuddled why their eyes couldn't see the lights anymore. Their minds thought that the world might end. Unknowingly, the dead leaves transformed into five letters and ten memoirs in the cave. These masterpieces looked like a dazzling star in the night. A million eyes were electrified to gaze at the contemplation, though their eyes were unable to find the superstar, still they were amazed how it grasped their nights.

What do you discover in the letters and memoirs?

Each verse is written by someone else for his/her secret admirer in Disneyland. Once these letters/memoirs will be discovered by the intended receiver. It could alter their lives and make it richer. All of their wishes will be given onto their hands, which leads to staying happy ever after. That night, ten people dreamt what they might find in the cave. It was talking about how to live their lives meaningfully and astoundingly.

That day, the people in the universe were madly in love with their dreams, indeed they craved to find those verses, to change their lives into richer and happier. Many people craved to stay in the cave, however one person was allowed to stay and visit each day in the cave.

As the people discovered the spectacular cave, their elegant eyes saw different colors each night. The moment they clipped their eyes to the surface, their minds clipped the entire heaven.

On the first day, *the world looked so blue, like the sea, which carried Abigaile's feet. A beautiful girl from another planet visited the earth, just to heal her blind eyes. Her sister just accompanied to stay with her, till Abigaile trudged to the cave. On the spot, the girl found a memoir from Kyle, a handsome man on the earth who had passed away a few years ago. That man gripped her over his dreams, however Abigaile slapped his eyes, which led to complicate Abigaile's eyes, what she did to him. As quoted by his memoir written by Kyle.*

To Abigaile

Life is like a tree, billions of eyes can see, yet a single eye clutched by the beautiful palm. However, the thorny hands crumpled the hills by your side. It's been a trillion nights of seeing you over my dreams, which made me shocked why the waves couldn't pull you over my hands.

I stood like dead soil on the land, still seeing you again over this letter. I can drench your eyes to view how bountiful the world is. What one thing I could tell you, it's nice to meet you again in my life. I heartily forgive you, Tonight, please allow me to grasp your hands, it will attach to my spirit till the end.

After her sister read the letter, Abigaile was able to read it with her eyes. Amazingly, she could see the enticing man who looked at her till the end. Being enticed by his eyes, it fell down her tears, casted back what she did to him. As she reread these verse**s,**

"What one thing I could tell you, it's nice to meet you again in my life. I heartily forgive you," Her eyes found the man again who gripped her hands," **I am sorry Abigale for holding you."** Then, she hugged him too, **"it's okay, Kyle,"** the more she hugged him, her hearts became peaceful and minds full of positive vibes. She wanted to extend more time with him, however the man had gone over her eyes. It's melancholy to know that she couldn't extend more journeys with him. Despite this, she felt chuffed that her eyes could see the great sunset and spectacular arts in the world.

There have been a few moments of dreaming Kyle, which made Abigaile contemplate bridging to him. Like how vital it is to bridge with her hands to anyone. Meanwhile, Kyle was unable to see her, still he often carried her on the way, just to make Abigaile's life happy.

On the second day, the world looked like a green leaf in the sky. The moment Andrei stared at the universe, his eyes rewrote how sweet his journey with Kylee Shane was. His eyes attached to the sun, just to ask for a second chance of meeting his beloved girlfriend again.

Looking back at the past, Andrei lost his hope to survive after the trials had passed in life. Like his girlfriend who often inspired him to stay happy, indeed he made his life meaningful. Endless nights of being part of her arms, which kept on growing his mind like the green leaf. Unfortunately, Kyle Shane got in an accident which altered his life, indeed he didn't see any positive things to his life. Though it had happened a few years ago, still he longed to hug Kylee Shane again.

Every time he stared at the window, his eyes drenched Kylee's smile, which made him cry. His tears were like a river, which fell down in the bay. Though he pledged to put his tears over the clouds, still his eyes gripped the beautiful smile, what Kylee Shane showed to him.

That night, Andrei had travelled the entire universe, his eyes gazed at the lovely star that fell down; it was really similar how exquisite the girl was. Can't deny, he missed her the most, however the falling star shut in the cave.

Despite that, Andrei finally arrived in the crust; his eyes found nothing, except the memoir fell down at his eyes. As he put his mind on the verses, it shuddered his eyes, how the verses made his heart cool. He wished to hug her for a thousand nights till the end of his life.

To my handsome man,

Seeing the way is enough, which rampled the day into a wonderful night. I can't imagine how you have changed my life. Though nobody cannot see me again,, how worthless I am after death. Still I perceive your smile to my garden, where I often feel your lovely arms.

I am gone by your enticing eyes, still the grasses be the honeyed sasshed.

"To stay with you again seems superfluous sun

All nights I often look the blank way

Still I envisioned how Andrei made my day

To be with you is the finest dream to carry the land

Gripping the verses, which made Andrei eyed on the past. That night, he reread the memoirs till his eyes found Kylee Shane again, who touched his clothes. Then, he fully hugged her arms till the clouds had gone in the universe. That night, Andrei uttered these verses,"

"To be with you is my finest dream to carry the sun."

"I can't let you go, since I can carry the land."

"My eyes enticed the tantalizing arts"

"Loving you is often be part"

"Holding you till the end"

"How I wish to be part of my garden"

Instead of leaving him tonight, Andrei kept on uttering the verse," **all nights I often look the way, till you have made my day.."** Then, he attempted to carry the land using his left hand which transformed Kylee Shane into a beautiful woman, who left her death, just to stay with him again all the nights.

"Let me hold the sea"

As long as eyes could see"

"The rhyming verses pulled the way"

"Still Andrei is my day"

The more Andrei saw over his eyes, enticing feelings often attached to her. Indeed, a day couldn't be a flawless May until he looked at Kylee's bay.

On the third day, the world looks red in the sky. The moment, Tiffany is one of the most beautiful creatures in the universe. She wants to be loved by the man who holds her over the thousand waves. To know more about her, she's the goddess in heaven where she has been living for three hundred years. One of her wishes is to have a man who will be the right medicine and be her forever friend. She often wishes for Tyler, the handsome God in the kingdom of Nymph to give her wishes. However, the God won't give it to her, due to his secret feelings to the enchanting Goddess. He does feel afraid to let her know, due to Tiffany's terrible impression of him. With that, Tiffany never had a great peace of mind, there might be times when Goddess 's body looked like a dead person in the kingdom of Nymph. As part of their culture, once she won't produce a child; the universe will turn into a salt.

Tyler casted back what might happen, once Goddess would have turned into a salt. Hence, he transformed his body into a dead leaf. Tiffany's eyes were enticed by the dead leaf over her dreams. She asked why she liked it the most.

Seeing the red lights in the sky, it pulled Tiffany's feet to visit the cave. Her mind envisioned how lovely the night would be to stay there. She didn't want to find the right man to love her. However, he longed to know the connotation of red lights in the sky.

As she was trolling on the feet of the cave, she also found a memoir which made him excited to read the verses. It was written by Tyler exclusively for her.

To Tiffany,
Indelibly Gripped the Night, just for You

A spectacular flower is like the art in heaven.
Nothing to get enticed, except by its ailes
As a fantastic as a tale
Where irresistible waves often scream

All nights quivered the dulcet bay,
Honeyed sea indelibly as blind as I eyed the day
I know how to let you go, still nothing can't be
As often I vision about you

For sure, you haven't know
I often wish to be the best as new
Still you had expunged the clouds
Where I can write the tears for you.

Am I so dreadful at your side?
As I trudge on the bay
Just to find you, yet you eyed nothing at me

Reading Tyler verses, Tiffany screamed over the hills; she wished to meet him again, just to ask for an apology. She wished to tell him why he disliked him. However, there's no time to do that for him.

As Tiffany trudged the cave, her tears wiped by the invisible hand. As she smiled after removing the tears, her heart became peaceful and healthier than before. While walking, she often gripped the verse, it was the best time to realize how important it is to appreciate what someone did to her. Despite that, she's happy that Tyler revealed to her," **I often stay by your side, even if you can't see me**," which is often attached to her heart.

All nights stay red like how Tyler secretly loved her. Unable to see him not to feel sorrowful, yet her heart is full of reddish arms. Being part of Tyler's memoir, it turned her into fruitful as it is.

On the fourth day, the world looked pink in the sky. This may let the eyes look back to the past, feeling so missed the day. Like Piolo, a caring man to his beloved mother. Being gripped by his mother's arms is countless moments to look back on, however there were nights swirled with his eyes. There were times of feeling hopeless in the sky, nobody could heal it, except his mother's arms.

It's been a million nights of being drenched by her mother, even if he's already 30 years old. Sadly, his mother had gone in the sea, where they talked about Piolo's secret feelings for Isabelle, a beautiful girl in the town.

This is one the saddest moments in life, though Piolo could stand by his feet. Indeed he trudged the hills by his wings, still he might paralyzed without his mother. Being dependent on his mom's arms is one of the best lessons that he learnt from his past.

There were a few moments not believing himself as he stayed alone. Both nights and days tears swallowed on the way..

His face seemed down to earth till Isabelle saw him. She let him know about the miracle in the cave.

"Trust me"

"Loving the arms can be found"

"Though dead seems nothing"

"Still a cave tells how to believe the thing"

His eyes glimpsed at the twilight which gripped his past. Uncovering the memorable story with his mom growing in his arms. Despite the terrible feelings that had happened to his life, still Piolo felt chuffed as he trudged on the cave, his eyes gazed at the pinkish lights. One of his wishes is to see and hold his mom again.

Alongside Piolo's arms, unexplainable feelings seeing the beauty and rhyme of the night. He ran away from Isabelle, as he gazed at the letter beside his arms.

Till to See You again

Eyeing you again, as amaranthine snow
Night can't pull my heart as thy pink jacket
Though I am not visible in thy eyes
A flawless garden glimpse us apart

All nights I longed to be
Like how thy gripped the honeyed day
Let the enticing night to grip again
I am not like a sun

Still a cloying night be thy can

No ever dreams I wish to come
Except, a lovely hand be cloying sand

Lovely,
Invisible mother

After reading the letter, Piolo gazed at his mommy, tears fell down upon touching her arms again. Feeling such a blast of seeing her again, when he looked back, how Isabelle found his mommy again.

He gripped his arms, "**I won't let you go,**" however the shadow had gone. He endlessly gripped his mommy, while he uttered these words," **be always my garden in the bay where I can see the source of arts and fantasy.**" His eyes swirled at the fantastic sight.

"'I' won't leave you, however life ends,"
"It's wrench to reveal this, yet swirled hands often stayed with you."
"O endless love gone, still hands will often be you."
"No world can be perfect, still loving you till does"

Countless tears fell down as the mother transformed into a dead leaf again. He craved to read the letter again, however the eyes won't see the way again. His eyes endlessly read the letter from his mom, though he just heard her voice like a tunnel.

As the night moved forward, Piolo stepped forward on his feet. One thing he couldn't forget was how Isabelle bridged him to visit the cave. One night, he met Isabelle in the park, he gripped his hands at her. It was the impeccable night to reveal their secrets, he let her know how thankful he was for her. He also told her how Isabelle put his arms above the hills. He offered himself to spend his nights with her.

That night, Isabelle let him know how much she was infatuated with him. However, she stood like a rainy day to him. Despite that, she put his eyes by her secret garden where feelings grew.

"Island is like an arm"

"Like how you alarm"

"Night is meaningless, not being you"

"All days I wish to write my feelings for you"

"Life will end, still to grow the arms, still be fine"

"Seeing you again is like a ton"

Despite this, the typhoon happened to his life in the town. Still Isabelle made a garden for him.

On the fifth night, inexplicable feelings seeing the arts in the hills and clouds, which looked yellow. The more Khian deeply bonked the color, the more enticed how truly his life was. Imagine, he lived his life like a wave on the sea, despite the thorns on the way. Looking back, he did terribly to his friend who had passed away.

In Disneyland, Khian craved to end his life. What he often printed over the hills, his life faced endless challenges like having a dreadful face as a dog, and a little height of five inches. Imagine, he lived like a hen in the village, the more the thousand eyes put him down on the way, especially when folks saw his awful height and terrible face.

Most of the time, he shut his eyes in the sky, why he suffered in his life. Though he had a good health, he longed to skip his challenges. There have been times, invisible hands gripped at him. He just heard these statements," **look at the yellow sky while trudging on the way."** Then, a shadow passed by his way, which led to close his eyes for a day.

As he woke up, eyes saw the arts in the cave. It seemed yellow, captured by his eyes, seeing that color. He felt optimistic to see the meaning of his life.

As he moved forward, the two leaves fell down and carried his arms. The moment he laughed, the leaves transformed into letters, which climbed over his hands. That night, he put his eyes on the verses;

To you, Khian,

Life is full of waves, like how you passed by. However, you forgot to look back on your past. Did you still remember what you did to your friend? Angel Gabriel is your best friend, right?

She's still your friend, however you were the reason why she didn't meet you again. Due to uttering offensive words at the back of her, which made Angel Gabriel got offended by your words. As part of the tales, your awful height and face will alter, once you heal her painful hearts.

"I often treated more than friends"

"Like how I grip the leaf not to fall"

"Still the clouds dull"

"I am still your friend"

"Words like a tale"

"How it cut the pale"

After putting his eyes on the letter, his mind casted back what he did to Angel Gabriel. It's been a decade since Angel hurt his words. His heart screamed how to hold her again, as he turned at the right side. He noticed an angel who flew down beside him. The angel acted like a Goddess in heaven, seeing him in the sky; Khian screamed what he did to her.

"Seeing you again makes me happy"

"Let me erase the hurtful words which grow in your heart"

"Nothing I could say, so sorry"

"A hand endlessly raise, just to find you"

Then, Angel Gabriel crossed her hands at him. Being attached by her hands, Khian craved to hold her till the end of his life. The more to utter an apology," let me rewrite the terrible letters in the sky." Then, he hugged her like how he gripped his enticing dreams.

Seeing his genuine words, Angel Gabriel swirled the thousand words gripped at Khian's hands.

To you, my finest friend,

"Past is past"
"Often destroyed the sand"
"I stood like Angel in heaven"
"Undying bough I truly done"
"Death inveigle the garden"
"Life stood like a dazzling bay"
"Where an impeccable night grows as fresh leaf"
"Letting you know, a heart runs as peace as sniff"

Then, Angel tightly gripped his cloying shoulder, which made Khian's appearance transformed into a handsome man. Indeed, Angel liked what the eyes sniffed at him. She craved to enjoy her nights with him, yet she didn't feel hurt again.

On the sixth night, the world brimmed with green lights in the universe, which grasped the folks' eyes. Captivatingly, the man fascinated glancing at the dazzling light, though Jariv, a bewitching doctor, lost his hope to continue his profession, due to the unsuccessful operation of his patient.

The folks lost their trust to him, which had pulled his confidence in the fire. Endless nights, Jariv painfully carried the tears in the sky. In the town, rain never ceased, due to his tears which often fell down on the ground. It's indeed hurtful to carry the excruciating land.

As the green lights flashed its superb silver to his eyes, which Jariv deeply read the hopeful verses;

A worth life is like a stone

Shined all the way

Till the day be thy May

Like how Jariv rewrite the fantasy

Though hands fails

Still a scintillating leaf often prevail

It's been a hundred nights of gripping the verses over his eyes till he slept in the bed. Filled with fleshed moments laying down like the sea. As he woke up, his elegant eyes glanced at the cave, where he saw the green leaf. He just bonked the leaf, surprisingly, it converted into a lovely memoir.

"Seeing your tears like I often hold the waves"

"Though the operation was unsuccessful as dead"

"Always put it onto mind, life is like a play"

"Run like a car"

"Surely, I often be your scars"

He attempted to run on the cave which led to develop his confidence again. Indeed he craved to go back to his profession again. All nights, he read the memoir which was written by someone else. One of his wishes is to hold the hand which captivatingly wrote the memoir for him.

Due to excitement, Jariv explored the entire cave till the green lights had gone. However, his eyes drenched at the lovely letter from his ex-lover.

To you, Jariv, my unforgettable man,

Life is full of memories, which I gripped over the sun

It's been a year of not eyeing you

A letter seems indelible as sand
I truly trolled the way
Yet, you pull me on the sea

Best memories,
Patrizha

    After reading the letter, his mind printed back on the hills. Patriza screamed how terrible Jariv did to him. To tell the story short, Jariv left her, just to focus on his profession as a medical doctor. There was a misunderstanding between their ways, despite that the memoir is still indelible. If the rainbow won't be deleted, the remarkable memories can't be.

Before the night ends, Jariv endlessly wishes to meet Patrizha again, just to expound why he left her one decade ago. Meanwhile, Patriza slept on her bed, yet the green leaf fell down over her eyes.

To Ms. Patrizha,

    Memory can be written in the stars
Where I often whiffed the candied days!
    Loving you is like an astounding flee
No matter how far
I often be your car
Let my hands be gripped the sand
Like how Jariv inveigle the land

Lovely regards,
Jariv

Everytime Patrizha read the letter. Her mind printed the fantastic tales, which gripped over the hills. As she woke up, the sea pulled her out where Jariv bridged his thrilling nights for her. She couldn't delete the rainbow, yet Jariv's hands carried her over the sea, just to carry their lovely day.

On the seventh night, *the world boozled with orange lights, which astoundingly materialized in the sky. It's been a million days of drinking wine with his friends, due to less love from his family. Mark Justin, a charming man in the town. He's gifted when it comes to painting and logic. Indeed he's famous in the University.*

However, Mark Justin took it as worthless, due to withered love from his family. Instead of finishing his college, he truly painted his moments with his friends for a billion nights. He often trusted them more than his family.

That night, one of his best friends sold him to Cayzer, an invisible vampire in the town. It took a thousand nights of sleeping in the bed till Mark Justin woke up. His eyes were deeply petrified seeing the blood beside him, just hearing the horrifying voice. He roared loudly, just to be saved by his mommy.

The more he shouted, the more the invisible vampire gripped him, " **learn to forget your friends, I can be your friend**.*" And then, the vampire showed her enticing eyes at him.*

"Let me put you over the green tea"

"Wherever a flawless grasses can be"

"Time is like a cross where the trust lost"

"A truly love, a lovely night never be yours"

That night, Mark Justin frankly told her that he hankered to go back to his town nor to stay with her. Cayzer never allowed him to troll on the way, yet his appearance was filled with blood like a pure vampire. That night, the man regretted that he trusted his friend.

Due to the countless tears fell down from his eyes. Unexpectedly, an orange leaf fell down over his face. The leaf transformed into an exquisite girl, Mhaven, one of the exquisite creatures in the kingdom. Her tantalizing hands wiped Mark Justin's tears, which were undyingly indelible to his memory. However, the queen has moderately gone from his eyes.

He has been dreaming of holding her hands, just to cease his tears. There have been moments of glimpsing her beautiful eyes. Meanwhile, a comely voice whispered to his aisles.

"Loving the family is like holding the star"
"Rain or shine cramped over the leaf"
"At least, family never pull out the sea"

These verses let him go back to his past. He learnt not to trust his friend, but to love his family, no matter what. One night, his eyes saw the orange lights, he attempted to ride it, which led him to trudge the cave. He wished that his appearance would return to original face.

Here, the man found the dead leaf, however his eyes enticed the letter. This is written by Mhaven for him. A beautiful queen at Ariel's kingdom.

To you, Mark Justin,

"Leaf can be painted by the rainbow "
"However trust can be deleted"
"I often cling the heart, like how to flee"
"Yet, a cave is the best knee"
"Just put thy eyes on the letter"
"Where a fantastic life arise"
"Learn to swirled the odd stars "
"Where rich life as pearl as far"

Mark Justin contemplatively read the letter till his bloody image turned into a charming man again. He longed to stare at the woman who wrote these verses for him. Before sleeping he frequently read it till the letter transformed into an enchanting Queen. She eventually showed her appearance to him.

Seeing the queen, MJ felt electrified to grip the queen's hands. That time, the queen revealed that MJ's family had gone to the town. Screaming as he heard the news, which deleted the grasses on the ground.

Mhaven endlessly helped him to meet his family. After several nights, he finally met them, heartily hugged them, as his hands gripped the mountain. He pledged himself to alter his life, often loving his family nor friends. That time, the queen couldn't measure her gladness, as MJ met his family again.

He lived a peaceful life, however he missed the queen to go back to his life. He madly wished to hug her, how the queen had changed his life. It took a thousand nights of writing his memoir for her.

Due to the conflict in the kingdom, Mhaven was being destroyed by her king. Her image identical as snow, nobody could see her, except Mark Justin over his fetching eyes.

That night, MJ let his hands grip the snow; he just held the snow for a thousand nights. His hands felt how sweet the snow was, as he opened his irresistible eyes. Mark Justin surprisingly met the queen again, and was looking forward to spending more nights with her.

Mark Justin let the queen read the memoir, which he wrote for her.

To Queen Mhaven,

Being hills over the past nights

Tears might rain on the bay

Yet, a hidden arts painted

Let the sea be my day

As often I look how changed my life

As beautiful as the butterfly

Best memories,

Mark Justin

Reading his memoir, the queen deeply touched it. Indeed she rewrote it in the stars, till the end; the verse often be indelible and remarkable.

On the eight night, *the world filled with brown lights, which scattered on the way. Seeing the path, Elias, a honeyed artist in the garden where he placed his hurt aches and injustice in the world. One of the hurtful moments was when he put his crystal hearts on Dave, a sassy man in the town. A man who accepted his gender identity, no matter what.*

There have been electrifying moments to stay with him. However, Dave had a secret which he couldn't reveal to him. He craved to disclose it however he didn't want Elias to fall down the stairs.

Due to the brown lights flashing in their eyes, Elias and Dave went to the island, where they made an exciting moment. Unknowingly, Dave had a secret plan to skip from him.

In the middle of the night, Elias and Dave slept beside the wet spring. As the dawn materialized in the sky, Elias deeply glanced at the Alien, who slept beside him.

Looking at the terrible alien, Elias lost his self-esteem, indeed he got depressed about what had happened to his life. It's been a trillion nights of taking his sleep, due to his deep reflection about his life.

It's countless nights of seeing the brown lights. Without hesitation, he attempted to hold it, the lights carried his body to the cave, where he deeply mediated his life. Due to the frequent dead leaf passed by his arms, his eyes found a memory, which could be hooked his entire night.

His eyes twinkled reading the letter, which led to putting it onto his mind and heart.

Dear Elias,

Staying in your arms is one of the best moments, which I have been falling in with you. There has been a thrilling moment of putting the snow together, which quaked the aisles. This letter let me write the lovely words, why I left you.

I have planted my secret for you. I am not a real man, my gender is always the same as yours. Happiness can be found in you, yet I won't let you discourage what I have.

To end this,
Elias often swirled the island
Where Dave enticed the can
Irresistible nights pull the exciting bay
Let the romantic hands be the way

Loving you is like gripping the star
Rain or shine, a ship rummage the sea
Yet, an invisible sun often the key
To see you again whiff afar

Farewell,
Dave

    After reading the letter which was written by Dave exclusively for Elias. This has helped him to stop loving without knowing the person's life. As he trudged the cave, he printed these words onto his mind. Though he finally accepted the reality, indeed he put peace into his mind. Now on, Elias lived a better life than before.

On the ninth day, *the world looked purple, which made Cedric electrified, a soul, he wished to go back to his original life. Seeing the lights, it vividly drenched him, to hug Tina, a beautiful girl, who has been loving for him since they were young.*

Casting back to the past, Cedric craved to leave his death. Endless regret why he didn't spend more time with her. Secretly, Tina, a vampire killed him, due to her secret, she didn't want to reveal it to him that she was pregnant, not from him.

Tina's eyes fell down, as he stared at the purple lights that night, till she became ash.

As she faced the thorns of her life, she often remembered how essential Cedric was. Anytime, the ash kept falling on different hills, no peace and nobody would like to hold it, except Cedric.

There have been times, the ash flew down on the cave, which attached to the dead leaf. Due to the hurtful deeds, the ash transformed into a letter.

That night, Cydric's eyes endlessly trudged in the sky, till his eyes deeply attached the letters, which had been reflected from the cave. The moment the purple's lights twisted. The more the letter emerged in the sky.

Rain fell down, then a letter attached at Cydric's eyes;

Devil wrenched on the way

Like how I lost the day

Endless bloods ran on the river as you, Cedric

No word can describe me, except demon

I can't describe you how sweet you are

Still, a hand pulled me to be a Satan

"Once again, I am sorry Cedric for taking your life. I am not a rain to make you alive again. Still I regret why I assassinated you."

Revealing what Tina did to him, which made Cedric realised to stop wishing to go back to his original life. It's been a billion times of seeking Cedric till she found him.

It's a perfect time to grip his hands, however Cedric didn't accept it anymore. That night, Tina endlessly fell down her tears, she craved to be loved by Cedric again. However, a thorny wind touched her.

"Loving you again is a blessing, yet a harmful pain can't be a garden. It's been a thousand nights of wishing to grip you again. However, no words can be planted in my garden, as often, loving you till the end. Still my heart needs to renew."

Tina endlessly grips him, just the man to go back, yet the purple light has gone, as Cedric's feelings fade away.

On the tenth night, *the world brimmed with gray lights both hills and sky. Walking the way, Dave, a handsome engineer, eyed the enchanting white lady beside the tree. He felt befuddled why his way seemed bloody. He is still working in the workplace, yet his eyes are unable to find the right way, just to leave the white lady.*

That white lady enticed how Dave built the house uniquely. Her main intention was to build a house for her tribe. Here, he showed his talents to her, which made the white lady believe that Dave can do it.

It's been ten nights, Mercy not seeing her friend. Her colleagues worried about what might happen to Dave. Instead of crying, Mercy went to the CCTV camera, just to see where Dave went. Unfortunately, she was unable to find it.

Well, Mercy went back to the cave, just to open her wish. Here, she clamped her eyes to the dead leaf, what she glimpsed at, Dave seemed happy of his life in the Milky Way.

That time, Dave missed his friend, not just to see her, but how Mercy inspired him in his life. His eyes found the magical key, which had helped him to open his world again.

However, Dave was unable to see his friend again, which led him to live alone. One day, a leaf fell down over his eyes, as he trudged it. The leaf transformed into a memoir;

Tears can be written in the lane
How I miss you, as I wish to feel the same
Nothing I feel, except to make you feel the over moon
I trudge the hills, how the clouds put me into a spoon

It's just a few lines, still Dave put it over his mind. He lived alone till decided to visit the cave; his eyes enticed the memoir again," as you had left in the Milky Way, no way seems fine. Seeing your unique painting, my heart often remembers you. "

That night, Dave put the memoir over his arms, where the white lady stayed till the end. He joined her in the invisible place, where he eventually knew the white lady was his friend.

-Ends-

About the Author

Ariel C. Cabasag

Ariel has been working as an English instructor and creative writer for almost six years in the Philippines. He's a man who loves letters and language, which really helps me to transform his imagination through creative writing. To him, life is meaningful and worthwhile, as he has expressed himself through writing such masterpieces in English literature.

In addition to that, he's famous insttuctor in teaching English communication, which further drives him to showcase his talents in poetry and essay writing. Most of his students was really inspired by his talents; indeed, he has received many appreciation letters in teaching.

With regards to his educational background, he took MA in Teaching English Language and Literature at Ateneo University, where he further learned the language. And got idolized some effective professors, who indeed motivated him to love teaching English language. After a year, he became a professor at Far Eastern University, where he published many poems: green letters in the cave and whisle in the milky way. Meanwhile, he started his second MA in Literary and Cultural Studies at Ateneo de Manila, where he further enhanced his talents in writing: to become globally competive both writing care.

www.ingramcontent.com/pod-product-compliance
Lightning Source LLC
LaVergne TN
LVHW041602070526
838199LV00046B/2105